D1392450

Snug as a Bug

For Ethan,
the snuggliest bug of all
– *TM*

To my little boy Mattia
–*JA*

SIMON AND SCHUSTER

First published in Great Britain in 2013 by Simon and Schuster UK Ltd

1st Floor, 222 Gray's Inn Road, London WC1X 8HB

A CBS Company

Text copyright © 2013 Tamsyn Murray
Illustrations copyright © 2013 Giuditta Gaviraghi

The right of Tamsyn Murray and Giuditta Gaviraghi to be identified as the author and illustrator of
this work has been asserted by them in accordance with the Copyright, Designs and Patents Act, 1988
All rights reserved, including the right of reproduction in whole or in part in any form
A CIP catalogue record for this book is available from the British Library upon request

ISBN: 978-0-85707-108-8 (HB)
ISBN: 978-1-47115-813-1 (PB)
ISBN: 978-0-85707-893-3 (eBook)

Printed in China
4 6 8 10 9 7 5 3

Snug as a Bug

Tamsyn Murray & Judi Abbot

SIMON AND SCHUSTER
London   New York   Sydney   Toronto   New Delhi

The morning was grey,
    it was gloomy and dark,
when George and his mum
    got dressed for the park.

George folded his arms
and started complaining,
"It's nasty and cold,
and – look! – now it's raining!"

Mum gave a big smile.
"There may be some puddles,
so just to be safe
I've packed extra cuddles."

"You'll be as snug as a bug
rolled up in a rug,

like **two** cosy bats
in thick woolly hats.

As hot as **three** pigs
in big purple wigs,

wrapped up like **four** llamas in stripy pyjamas.

As warm as **five** gnus in green furry shoes,

or **six** sizzling goats
in red overcoats.

Like **seven** great apes
in long velvet capes,

or **eight** flapping kippers
in leopard spot slippers.

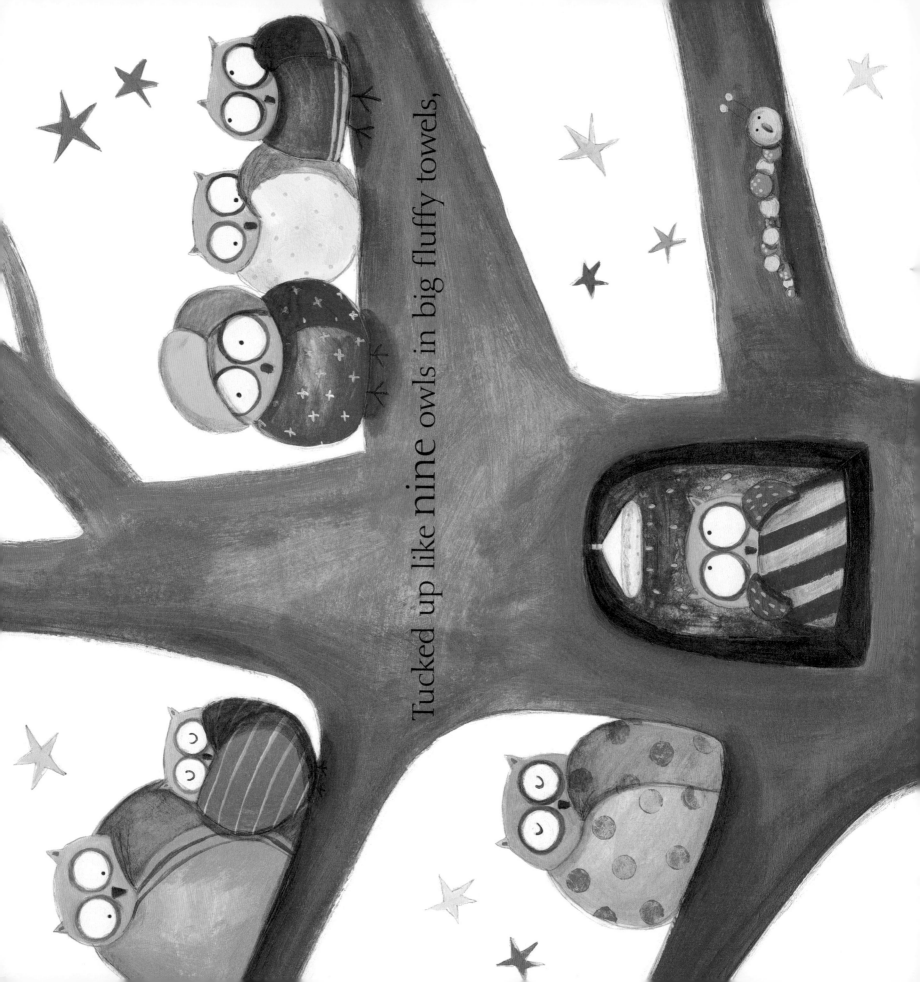

Tucked up like nine owls in big fluffy towels,

or ten toasty geese all sharing one fleece."

The park was such fun,
   it made George decide
to take off his coat
   as he went down the slide!

"Oh no," said his mum.
"Without that you might
get goosebumps or chills
or even frostbite!"

"You'll be like ten sneezy kittens without any mittens,

or nine frozen frogs
in huge wooden clogs.

As cold as **eight** bees
on miniature skis,

like **seven** long snakes
with icy milkshakes.

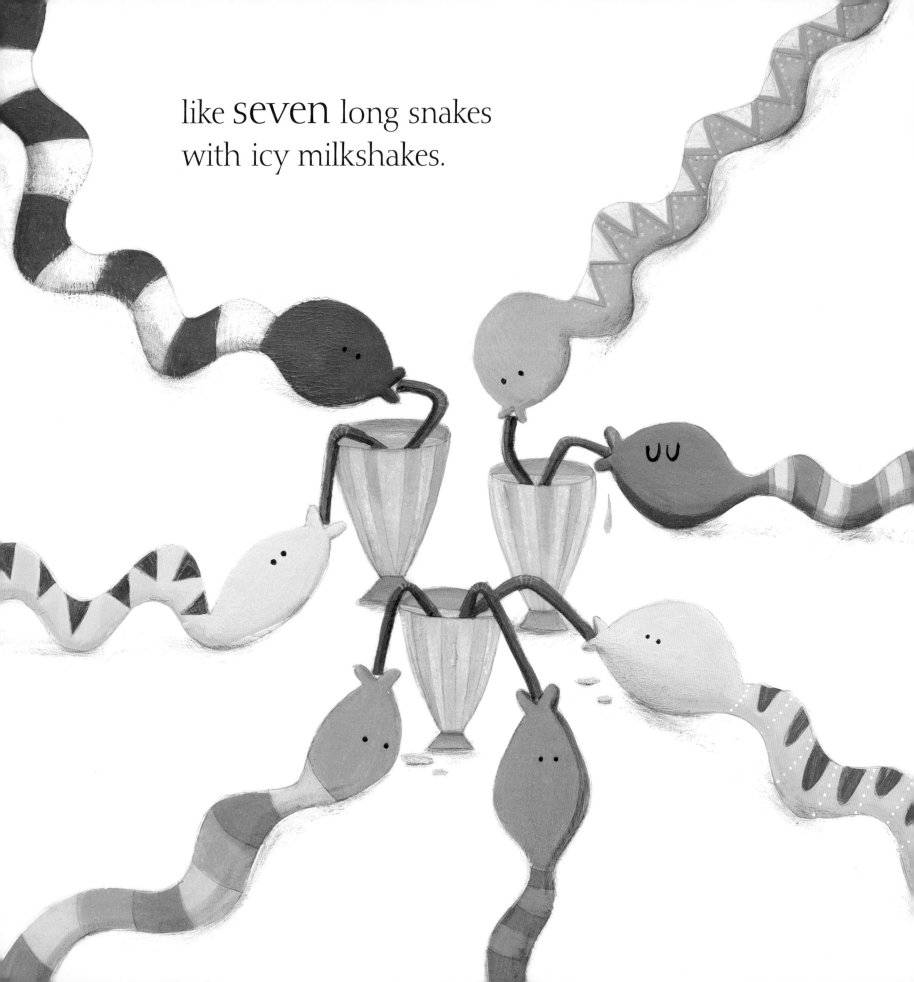

As chilled as six snails
caught out in the gales,

or five fancy ants
in sparkly hotpants.

Like four polar bears
with tears in their flares,

as cool as **three** mice in skates on the ice.

Like two tall giraffes
with snowflakes for scarves,

or one freezy fox
with holes in his socks."

George thought very hard,
   he rubbed at his nose.
"Mummy, I'm cold
      from my head to my toes!"

Mum pulled on his coat.
    Her eyes shone with twinkles.
"So now's not the time
    for ice cream with sprinkles?"

Tucked up that evening, George gave Mum a hug.

"I think I prefer being . . .

snug as a bug!"